Emily's Vow

A More Perfect Union Series Book 1

Betty Bolté

www.MysticOwlPublishing.com

later in the evening. With the press of so many bodies during the middle of the day, Evelyn had decreed no additional heat necessary. She'd been right, too. The doors and windows stood open to let in the cold January air, helping to mitigate the warmth created by the crush of guests.

The ladies had chosen beautiful gowns of their own for this special day. Cousin Emily's pale yellow gown suited her to perfection, with white roses embroidered around the scooped neck of the bodice and then reaching out in rays down the skirts. She wore her blonde curls in an smooth bun beneath a matching pale yellow hat made from lace and decorated with real white roses. Amy wore a midnight blue dress overlaid with lavender netting. Her dark locks had been tamed into an intricate hairdo, a few curls left to hang beside her rosy cheeks. Samantha, her new friend and adopted sister, had boldly chosen an emerald velvet gown, with a deep plunge of the neck and scattering of rhinestones across the bodice, which suited her coloring and green eyes. Her ebony hair had been fashioned into an elegant braid for the occasion, with wisps of curls left to dance about her face. Gold bobs hung on her earlobes and a matching chain graced her neck. A lovely trio indeed.

"Evelyn, I cannot thank you enough for your efforts to make the house so beautiful and welcoming." Emily drew her husband Frank Thomson closer to stand with her at Evelyn's side. "Everyone is talking about the beautiful flowers and ribbons, oh, and the array of branched candlesticks."

"You created a beautiful and romantic setting for our special day." Amy lightly hugged Evelyn, careful to not wake the baby. "A simple thank you cannot convey the depth of my gratitude. Especially after the terrible losses you've endured over the past month or so."

Amy's comment raised the memory of the gun shots, the violence, and the violations Evelyn had experienced. Her late husband Walter had been a difficult man to please. When she had not produced an heir within a few months of their marriage, he'd turned violent. Fortunately, she conceived a baby and his tirades abated. Until the renegades and scouts took turns scavenging the property. He held his tongue while the invaders took all they wanted, but then he had unleashed his anger upon her. She sniffed and shook off the misery threatening to dampen her spirits. She wouldn't permit anything to interfere with her happiness on her sister's wedding day.

"One must look to the future and move on when adversity strikes." Evelyn joggled Jim as he began to stir. Soon he'd be wide awake and hungry. He must be her focus, not the death of her abusive husband, nor the conflagration that consumed their manor house. Looking forward meant figuring out how she'd provide for her own household.

"I'm pleased you chose to accept our parents' offer. Since I'm moving out soon, they would be lonely without having one of us with them." Amy clasped her hands before her as she nodded. "It's some form of a miracle our father's finances are sound after all of the trials he's been through over the course of the war."

"Indeed. I'm fortunate they do not mind my return to their house." But Evelyn minded, more than she'd shared with any one. Her first task was to find her own place to live and raise her son. But how could she afford a house? The money Walter had set aside would last a few months with the current rate of inflation and the devaluation of paper money. Then what?

"At least you have a roof over your head." Nathaniel shifted his weight, closing the distance between them so his hip nearly touched hers. "I've just arrived in town and must find lodgings until I can locate a suitable domicile."

"I'm certain someone will open their home to you."

His nearness sent shivers through Evelyn's midriff. He exuded a force she sensed but couldn't define, one tempting her to touch him. What was wrong with her? She barely knew him. She took a half step away, covering her movement with a peek at Jim.

"We're a friendly city, now that the bloody Britons have departed." Frank slipped his arm around Emily's waist. "What do you think of having a guest?"

Emily glanced at Evelyn and then back to Frank. "If he'd like to stay with us, I'm sure we can make him comfortable."

Nathaniel inclined his head in thanks. "Very kind of you. But, what about your honeymoon?"

Frank shook his head, his blond hair neatly held in a queue for the occasion. "We've decided to remain at home and enjoy our newly refurbished abode instead of traveling at this time of year. But in a little while, we will make a journey."

"All the more reason for me to decline your generous offer." Nathaniel shrugged as he glanced at Emily. "I wouldn't wish to interfere with a newly married couple."

Trent raised both brows and shook his head. "Do not worry. We'll help you find lodgings. Perhaps Captain Sullivan will have a place, like he did for Benjamin."

"Nonsense, my friend. What of southern hospitality? Mr. Williams, you are welcome to stay with us. Isn't he, dear?" Benjamin peered at Amy. He was tall, dark haired, and handsome in an elaborately embroidered waistcoat peeking out from under a bright blue coat and trousers. Amy slowly nodded, doubt in her eyes. "See? We'd be pleased for you to share our house as long as you might need."

A host of conflicting emotions flashed across Nathaniel's face before he shook his head. "I appreciate the offer, but I simply cannot believe the newly married would wish a stranger in their midst. I'm sure if I were in your shoes I'd be reluctant to entertain guests."

Evelyn avoided meeting Nathaniel's eyes as he contemplated her with his last words. She hugged Jim close, her cheeks warming under his regard, and looked anywhere but in his direction. He seemed to hint at the underlying meaning of his words to her, provoking the tumult raging in her mind. She needed to remove herself from his presence and soon.

"That is a valid point." Benjamin grinned at Nathaniel. "It may be hard to sleep nights."

Amy swatted Benjamin's arm, blushing as his meaning spread through the group. "Mind your manners."

"Where will you stay then? If you won't stay with any of us, I mean." Samantha clasped her husband Trent Cunningham's arm as her gaze shifted from one to another of the group.

Evelyn liked Dr. Trent, and rejoiced that her dear friend had found the love of her life in the sandy haired handsome man. Like the others, Trent had donned his finest suit, the dark blue setting off his crystal blue eyes and a discreetly patterned waistcoat, both of which showed his strength and elegant carriage.

The rustle of taffeta and thump of leather shoes on the wood floor drew Evelyn's attention to the elderly couple approaching. Her parents, Richard and Lucille Abernathy, had aged gracefully, though her mother's ramrod straight back had bowed a little more each year. Their love revealed itself through the angling of their bodies toward each other as well as the looks they shared. Evelyn quickly made the appropriate introductions once they came to a halt.

If she could one day find a man who would treat her with the same respect and concern as her father shared with her mother, she'd be content. But the pickings proved slim after so many men had lost their lives securing the independence of America from British tyranny. Societal expectations weighed on her mind. She should find another husband, one to provide for her two-month-old son. If she only had herself to support, she'd manage with sewing or perhaps by being a governess. Jim, her mother had reminded her, needed a father to teach the boy how to be a man, and to ensure he received the requisite care and education to grow to his full maturity. Yet part of her wished to remain unmarried, independent of the needs and demands of a husband. But even knowing of the dearth of eligible bachelors, the next time she accepted a man's attentions, she'd be very careful and certain of his personality. She'd promised herself no one would hurt her ever again.

"I couldn't help but overhear. We have room for you and no recently wed occupants to worry about." Richard Abernathy slapped Nathaniel on the back. "Interested?"

Nathaniel smiled, his attention flicking her way and then back to her father. Evelyn held her breath, squeezing Jim until his murmur of protest made her relax her grip. Would this man be staying under the same roof? She desired distance between them, and suddenly the absolute opposite results hovered in the air. Definitely time for her to find another place to reside.

Nathaniel studied her for two beats of her heart before turning and stretching out his hand to shake with her father. "I'd be honored to accept, as long as it does not inconvenience any one."

"Not at all. If you'd like, you can ride in the carriage with us back to the house." Richard rested his large hand at the small of Lucille's back. "We intend to leave in a little while. We tire easily as the years go by, so we're off to say our farewells and then we can depart."

"Very good." Nathaniel nodded to Richard as he led his wife away, then fixed his attention on Evelyn. "Do you mind that I accepted your father's offer? I have no wish to make you uncomfortable in your own home."

"Why would I mind?" Evelyn kept her eyes on the handsome yet dangerous man regarding her with a serious expression. Dangerous first with regard to the scars he'd suffered during the fighting, indicating he resorted to aggressive behavior when pressed. Dangerous in that he'd also been a party to the raid on her house, a violent invasion of her home by the American militia in search of sustenance for the soldiers. Finally, dangerous to her equilibrium by his presence and his belief that fate had brought them together that scary day last fall during the raid on her home. She straightened her back, stiffening her resolve at the same time. Handsome is as handsome does, after all. "As long as you keep to yourself, we shall get along."

He nodded slowly but his charming smile slipped back into place. "I shall endeavor to honor your request."

"See that you do." A flicker of humor flashed in his eyes and she drew in a breath. "I'm in mourning, so your attentions would be, if not welcome, at best inappropriate."

The sparkle in his eyes went out. "I see."

Amy took Benjamin's hand in hers as she addressed Evelyn. "My dear sister, you, of all people, know how fearful it is to be without a home to live in. Now that your worries are behind you, please don't begrudge the young man shelter from the elements for a short stay while he makes other arrangements."

Evelyn angled her head and frowned at her sister. "What do you mean, my worries are behind me?"

"Why, you have a home and the security of our father's fortune to provide for you and your son." Amy waved a hand in the space between them. "You need not trouble your head about where and how you'll live. It's been decided."

Surprise swept through Evelyn. "No, it has not been decided." She espied doubt on the faces of her friends. "I have no intention of living with my parents for long."

Nathaniel nodded at her. "Looks like we have something in common."

Evelyn opened her mouth to contradict his claim, but Amy cut into the conversation.

"Look, Benjamin, Mr. and Mrs. Walters are preparing to leave. We must go thank them for their wedding gifts." Amy tugged on Benjamin's arm, drawing him away from the cluster of friends.

"Will you excuse us?" Benjamin addressed the group at large as he allowed Amy to pull him along behind her.

"Be off with you." Evelyn waved the three couples on their way. "We'll catch up with you later."

"Thanks again for all your help, Evelyn," Samantha said as Trent proffered his arm.

"My pleasure." Evelyn shooed them with a happy chuckle. "Go. See to your guests."

After the chattering friends had blended into the surrounding crowd, Evelyn turned back to Nathaniel. "So, Mr. Williams, will you be staying in town long?"

"I'm not sure. It depends on what Major Hanson has to say to-morrow when we meet." He peered at her, and a gentle smile emerged on his lips. "And what a certain recent widow might have to say as well. She may wish for me to dawdle in procuring my own residence."

Evelyn raised one brow at the provocative suggestion and then shook her head. She had absolutely no intention of beginning her husband hunt so soon after becoming widowed. "Do not depend on such an unlikely occurrence, Mr. Williams."

"Please, my friends all call me Nat. And I shall call you Lyn." He chuckled and folded his arms. "Since we'll be living under the same roof for a time, we may as well be friends."

Evelyn blinked at the man, astonished at the level of his audacity and yet drawn to him like the tide by the moon.

Yes, he was definitely a dangerous man. No one had ever shortened her given name into a nickname. Especially not a pet name that sounded so divine on his lips. She couldn't let him use the nickname if she had any hope of keeping him at a distance. "Please, call me Mrs. Hamilton, and I will call you Mr. Williams."

He shook his head, as though sad to correct her. "I think not. Lyn suits you exquisitely better."

Clearly, he couldn't be reasoned with, intent on having his way, much like Walter, who had cowed her into doing everything to please him. But no matter what she did or how she behaved, she had never really satisfied her husband. Except maybe in having a son. A son she'd do everything in her power to protect. Squaring her shoulders, she blinked at Nathaniel. She would not travel the path of subjugation ever again.

"I have never answered to a nickname, so if you intend to be friendly, you'll respect my wishes." She snugged Jim closer to her, preparing to walk away from the charged space suddenly stretching between them.

Nathaniel smiled at her, and made the beginning of a bow before straightening, glee in his eyes. "If you insist."

"I do." The mischievous smirk on his lips did not bode well. She'd seen his type before. She would make certain he behaved properly toward her.

Her young maid appeared out of the crowd. Dressed in her best frock, the black slave soon reached Evelyn's side and reached out to take Jim into her arms. "Want me to carry him? Your arms must be tiring."

"Yes, thank you, Jemma." Evelyn gladly transferred the weight of her son to the girl. "He may need a clean napkin, as well."

"I'll take good care of the young'un." Jemma rearranged the blanket over the wide awake boy. "You enjoy yourself, you here?"

Evelyn huffed a laugh as she fingered her skirts. "I have been, but now it's time we depart."

"Yes, miss." Jemma peered at the man beside Evelyn. "Is he coming with us?"

"It appears so. This is Nathaniel Williams." Evelyn glanced between the maid and the man. "My father invited him to stay with us for as long as he'd enjoy visiting."

"Pleased to meet you, Jemma." Nathaniel offered his bent arm to Evelyn, an invitation to his escort, but also the dubious invitation to touch him. "Shall we join your parents?"

His nearness set her heart racing. To lay her hand on his muscular arm would invite an undesired response. As much as she wanted to touch him, she could not permit herself to indulge the desire. She must tread carefully, and see he did as well. "As long as you remember you are a guest in our house, I will treat you with respect and deference." She had promises to keep, ones made to herself and to her son. Nothing would sway her from her mission. Not even tempting lips and an endearing smile. "I ask you to do the same."

"You have nothing to fear from me." He inclined his head and grinned at her when she gingerly rested the tips of her fingers on his coat sleeve.

The light yet electric touch of his arm, even through the sleeve, evoked a tiny gasp from deep inside her. Propriety kept her hand in place as they stepped off, making a path through the crowded rooms. They paused in an antechamber to don their warm cloaks and hats, avoiding further contact until he again crooked his arm. After pulling on her gloves, she reluctantly accepted.

As they approached her parents at the open front door, he glanced down at her. "I shall be on my very best behavior, Lyn."

She gaped at him. The challenge in his expression made her snap her mouth closed as they passed through the door and out onto the street. He dared her to accept his flirtation, a dare tempting and intriguing if worrisome. Her parents climbed into the conveyance as Nathaniel escorted her toward the vehicle. The corded muscles in his arm flexed beneath her tense fingers before he took her hand and helped her up into the waiting carriage.

She gathered her long skirts close as she sat on the cushioned bench seat, and then stifled a gasp when Nathaniel squeezed in beside her, Jemma and Jim on his other side. His leg rested against hers, hidden beneath the flap of his coat and her own voluminous skirts. With her parents sitting directly in front of her, calmly smiling and chatting with Nathaniel, she dared not draw attention to his impropriety. She pressed her lips together to keep from chastising him. Oh, she wished she'd been wrong, but she'd been so very right. He was indeed dangerous on all counts.

Betty Bolté is known for authentic and accurately researched American historical fiction with heart and supernatural romance novels. She has published more than 20 books of fiction and nonfiction topics. She earned a Master's Degree in English in 2008, emphasizing the study of literature and storytelling, and has judged numerous writing contests for both fiction and nonfiction.

www.ingramcontent.com/pod-product-compliance
Lightning Source LLC
Chambersburg PA
CBHW021116110726
47900CB00007B/2204